Lois-Ann Yamanaka

The Heart's Language

Illustrations by Aaron Jasinski

HYPERION BOOKS FOR CHILDREN
New York

Author's Note:

My husband, John, and I would like to extend our love and infinite thanks to the golden ones walking among us who have shared in our journey to cure our son's autism. And what is the cure for autism? We are certain that the truest cure begins with unconditional love. What we appreciate about those we wish to honor is that they recognized our sadness and strength in the battles for services, our despondency and hopes for JohnJohn's future, our successes and our failures as parents, our joys and our heartbreaks on a daily autism ride; none of them thought us saints; none of them saw our son's condition as a curse; all offered themselves in love and expertise and blessed us richly for it. John and I believed for a long time that JohnJohn chose us for his parents because we had the capacity to heal him and help him, flawed and imperfect as we both knew we were. But we now understand that he has come to teach and heal us, not the other way around. And he has come to teach all of those whose lives he touches: Grandma Jean and Grandpa Harry, Great-grandma Narikiyo, Aunty Mona, Uncle Shane, and wonderful Sammie, Aunty Kathy, Uncle Jeff, and best nephew/cousin Charlie, Aunty Carla Beth, Aunty Gladys and Uncle Daniel Yoon, Ross and Dustin Narikiyo; Aunty Charlene Nobriga, Ian and Ira, Charles Inferrera, Aunty Joanne, and Jessica Luahiwa; Aunty Claire Shimizu, Aunty Shari and the Nakamura family, Aunty Nancy Hoshida, Uncle Mel, Uncle Keoki Mercado, Mimi and Dede Spencer, Kenn Sakamoto, Linda Conroy, Uncle Don Sumada; Susan and Bert eating pipipi for pupu in Kalihi Valley; Donna Bray, Superb Editor; Morgan Blair, light; Zach Linmark, naptime in preschool; Cora Yee, artist wife; Patti Laba, Nana Mary, and the Sakai family; Robert and Doreen Teixeira, Corie and Travis; Tom and Trudi Cannon, BK; Tae, Sunhi, Jim, and Nora Okja Keller, Wing Tek Lum, Marie Hara, Joy and Xander Cintron, Laura and Albert Saijo, and our friends at Bamboo Ridge Press; Meredith and Hampton Carson; Verbano Friends Club, Mr. Verbano (Clyde Ramsey), Jeffrey Do, Eric Kahalelehua, Ken Fukunaga, Glenn Hirazawa and Jim Kang; Cary Tanaka, Michael Y. P. Chock, and Scott Storkamp; Dr. John Shih, Lynn Chang, Joanne Parrish, Aunty Faith, and staff at the Windward Infant and Toddler Program, Dr. Maggie Koven, Crisana Naomi Cook, and Faye Jones; Josie Woll, Dora Jean Ota, Marsha Akamu, Liz Watanabe, Nana, Grandma Maria, Aunty Karen, and the extended staff of the Sultan Easter Seals School; Mari Ann Arveson, Janice Simon, Pam Sakai, Kristi Lucas, Joy Sakai, Aunty Clara Kawasaki, Pauline Kokubun, Sharon Manner, Miss Mercedes, Cheryl Lamb, Kathy Mau, and everyone who cared for JohnJohn at Lanakila Elementary School; Aunty Katherine, Aunty Pali, Kathy Maemori, Marlene Inter, Miss Heidi, Miss Laura, Melissa Bunner, Miss Michiko Sato-Escobido, Toni Miyamoto, Nadine Okazawa, Haunani Domingo, Miss Suzanne B., Miss Mahina, Joyce, Mariah, Britney, Ms. Mossman, Makua Hanohano, Aunty Penny, Aunty Wanda, Alan Shimabukuro, Kathy Takaki, Alida Gandy, Dennis Dobies, and the staff and children at Kaiulani Elementary School; Patricia Yu, Miss Betty, Miss Suzie, Keoni Yago, Mrs. Abby Lyau, Mr. Blaine, Diane Suzuki, Carole Matsukawa, Brandi Nishimoto, John and June from Robert's Hawaii, Shane Tamantigan, Russell Nishimura, and the staff and students of Jarrett Middle School; S.T.A.R.T. Staff, Renee Nakama, Shahidrah Roberts, Joanne Smith, Ian Watanabe, Thomas Hansen, David Brown, Ian Lowland, Melissa Marquez, Michelle Manibong, and especially Mr. Reggie Dela Cruz; Aunty Sue and Uncle Lester Stigar; Holly Stepanuik, Karla Izuka, Deana Mirzah, Kristi Lane, Melinda Schram, Liz Plummer, Debbie Uyeda, Laurie Acohido, Janelle Li, Dr. William Bolman, Dr. William Sheehan, wonderful Boyd Slomoff; Joyce Allen and Vici, Cheyenne Akana and Beau, Sheila Kaimuloa and Matthew, Naomi Grossman and Vance, Leolinda Osorio, Mrs. Osorio, and Sonny; Joanne Beal, Amy, Tad, Genell, Ryan, Tomee, Kamaile, and all the friends at Booth Pool; Sandi Ishikawa, Rhonda Scott, Miss Marisa C., Aunty Roxanne, Dr. Kimo Chan, Dr. Sada Okumura; Mr. Mark, Gaston, and the beautiful children and staff at the Loveland Academy; Aunty Kui, Aunty Amy, and Hekili of Kualoa Ranch; Shizuko Ouwehand; our treasured students and families at Na'au: A Place of Learning and Healing; Caterine, Olivia, Na'i, Chiba, Toby, Dr. Lissa Kam, Darlene, and the Birdies; Aunty Bridget Kanaka'ole, Marlene, Kaleo and Lohi, Leo Richardson, Skye, Adam, Lisa Lawson, Dr. Errol Hamarat, Llewelleyn Smalley, the extended Kanaka 'ole ohana, and JohnJohn's beloved and trusted friend Nohea Kanaka'ole. So much love, Little Priest, so much love. Who would have thought this possible, to find in this mad world, so many who would take a little autistic boy by the hand, and with or without words, in ways both big and small, make him know that they understand and love him. God thought it possible. And so it was done.

Thank you,
LAY

Text copyright © 2005 by Lois-Ann Yamanaka
Illustrations copyright © 2005 by Aaron Jasinski
For information address Hyperion Books for Children, 114 Fifth Avenue, New York,
New York 10011-5690.
Printed in Singapore
First Edition
1 3 5 7 9 10 8 6 4 2
This book is set in Rotis.
Reinforced binding
ISBN 0-7868-1848-4
Library of Congress Cataloging-in-Publication Data on file.
Visit www.hyperionbooksforchildren.com.

For children who are challenged,
whose rich inner world sings,
whose longing for our understanding
requires of us the simplest
of human compassion.

For JohnJohn,
the Little Priest who came to heal.

For Mark Romoser,
hope manifest.
        —LAY

To my family for their continuous support,
encouragement, and friendship.
        —A.J.

There once was a boy who could speak to the trees—the ancient *koa*, *`ohi`a lehua*, and tiny *`ohelo*.

"Good morning," he said, his sound floating on a drizzle.

The trees answered in the turn of a leaf, the tip of a bud, and the opening of a blossom that tickled his face.

But the boy could not speak to other people. And other people could not understand the boy.

"No one in their right mind speaks to trees," the vegetable vendors gossiped at the open market.

The boy also spoke to the ocean.

"Wheee," he squealed into the ocean's gentle swoosh.

All the creatures of the vast sea answered. The hawksbill turtle swam to shore at the boy's sweet call. *Aholehole* sang from their sweeping silver school. And the smiling dolphins chirped his favorite songs.

But the boy could not speak to other people. And other people could not understand the boy.

"He cannot even tell you his name," a neighbor whispered. "Screaming and screeching like a wild animal."

The boy spoke to the birds of the rain forests.

"Hello," he said in thin notes carried on the wind.

The *pueo* of the highlands, *auku`u* of the watercress patch, and the Japanese white-eye on the *kwai fa* tree lifted their beautiful voices in response.

But the boy could not speak to other people. And other people could not understand the boy.

"He's not like the other children," his father worried.

"He's in his own strange little world," his mother sighed.

The boy spoke to the animals in his yard.

"I'm here," he said with a warm brush of his hand.

The huge dog brightened up and wagged his tail. The small cat rubbed against the boy's leg. And the neighing horse gave him a tender nudge.

But the boy could not speak to other people. And other people could not understand the boy.

How the boy longed to speak to people! He could hear all of their words. He knew their very thoughts.

He wanted to chat, to talk story, to shoot the breeze.

He wanted to laugh, to cry, to share his joy and his sadness, his fear and his hope. But no one knew how to listen to him.

He wanted to have a friend. Just one. But no one seemed to want to learn or even understand his language.

Most of all, he wanted to say "I love you" to his mother and father.

But the boy could not speak to other people. And other people could not understand the boy.

Tired and sad, the boy stood alone on a grassy hill. He had all but given up hope. He cried out from a place inside him, long and deep, like a woodwind's lonely breath. Then the boy lay down on the grass. He closed his eyes.

And all the world stood still.

Then from the branches of the ancient *koa*, the boy heard the pulsing of mighty wings. He opened his eyes to the falling of blue feathers around him.

The boy looked up into the sky and happily flapped his arms. The blue bird landed in a patch of fuzzy dandelions. The swirling of puffy seeds touched the boy's face like an angel's breath.

The boy and the blue bird settled side by side on a grassy hill.

"You called me with the language of your heart," the blue bird told the boy. "That is why I came."

The boy smiled.

"I know all of your wishes and dreams," the blue bird said. "I know how much you want to speak. I know how much you want a friend. I know how much you want to say 'I love you' to your mother and father."

The boy nodded.

"Speak with the language of your heart."

The boy opened his mouth. But nothing came out.

"Speak with the language of your heart," the blue bird said again.
   The boy nodded, because most of all, he wanted to say "I love you" to his mother and father. He opened his mouth again, but again, nothing came out.
   The boy began to cry.

The blue bird said nothing at first, then suddenly, he put the boy on his mighty back and flew him into the sky, following the sun.

"Speak from your heart just like the first time you called to me," the blue bird said, "and believe that they will hear you, because I heard you."

The boy closed his eyes and held on tight. The sunlight kissed his face.

Soon he began to speak with the language of his heart.

"Trees, good morning!" the boy called from the sky. The trees waved their branches in greeting.

"Sea friends, hello!" the boy called, coming through a beautiful pink cloud. And the ocean creatures chirped in response.

"Birds, hello!" the boy whistled as he flew over the rain forests.

"Animals, I'm coming home," the boy called to his hungry pets.

And then the boy saw his mother hanging the laundry in the dusty wind and his father pulling weeds in the vegetable garden.

"Mommy! Daddy!" he called. They turned to what they thought was their child's voice. But seeing no one, they returned to their chores.

The boy on the back of the mighty blue bird flew through a light rain.

The blue bird smiled at the boy. "You were heard."

The next day, the boy waited and waited for the blue bird on the grassy hill. But the blue bird never returned. When afternoon came, he heard his father feeding the animals. The boy watched the grassy hill outside his window. He saw his father's tired back heading toward the chicken yard.

Then the boy remembered how the blue bird taught him to speak with the language of his heart. "Mommy! Daddy!" he called.

His father stopped in the middle of his chores. His mother opened the door and sat next to him by the window. "Open," she said, placing her hands over her heart and his heart. "Please, let us learn your language." And for the first time, the boy's eyes met his mother's.

Then the boy flapped his arms. His mother flapped her arms.

And when the boy cried out from a place inside him, long and deep, like a woodwind's lonely breath, she cried out the same sound.

The trees, the ocean, the birds, the animals, the sun, the moon, and the stars began singing together. The boy's mother opened her eyes and listened to what sounded like a symphony. This was the first time she had heard the boy's language, because this was the first time she had listened.

The boy ran to the grassy hill. His mother and father followed him.

The boy pointed to the trees, who spoke to his mother and father in the tip of a bud, the spiral of a blossom, and the rustle of a branch.

The boy's mother and father heard the ocean sound of the hawksbill turtle, *aholehole*, and dolphin as they called to him.

They heard the singing of the *auku*`u, the Japanese white-eye, and the *pueo* as they flew overhead.

They heard the joy of the huge dog, the small cat, and the horse as they praised the boy's kindness.

The sun, the moon, the rains, the winds, and the stars began speaking all at once.

The boy's mother and father heard his language, because finally, they listened.

And on that grassy hill, the boy's words trembled in his heart, then moved to his lips. The boy opened his mouth like a soft bud. "I love you," the boy said softly, as the three words he longed to say flowed from him.